DON'T OPEN
THE DOOR!

DON'T OPEN THE DOOR!

Veronika Martenova Charles

Illustrated by David Parkins

Tundra Books

Text copyright © 2007 by Veronika Martenova Charles
Illustrations copyright © 2007 by David Parkins

Published in Canada by Tundra Books,
75 Sherbourne Street, Toronto, Ontario M5A 2P9

Published in the United States by Tundra Books of Northern New York,
P.O. Box 1030, Plattsburgh, New York 12901

Library of Congress Control Number: 2006903150

Library and Archives Canada Cataloguing in Publication

Charles, Veronika Martenova
        Don't open the door! / Veronika Martenova Charles ; [illustrated by]
David Parkins.

(Easy-to-read spooky tales)
ISBN 978–0–88776–779–1

        1. Horror tales, Canadian (English). 2. Children's stories, Canadian
(English). I. Parkins, David II. Charles, Veronika Martenova. Easy-to-read
spooky tales. III. Title.

PS8555.H42242D6 2007   jC813'.54   C2006–901937–1

ONTARIO ARTS COUNCIL
CONSEIL DES ARTS DE L'ONTARIO

We acknowledge the financial support of the Government of Canada through the Book
Publishing Industry Development Program (BPIDP) and that of the Government of
Ontario through the Ontario Media Development Corporation's Ontario Book Initiative.
We further acknowledge the support of the Canada Council for the Arts and the Ontario
Arts Council for our publishing program.

Printed and bound in Canada

1 2 3 4 5 6   12 11 10 09 08 07

CONTENTS

SLEEPOVER

PART 1

At last it was Friday.

Finally!

Tonight I had a sleepover

at my house.

First Leon arrived.

Then Marcos came.

We played my games

and I showed them

all of my treasures.

We traded cards, told jokes,

and made funny faces.

Then we pretended to fight,

like in a movie.

My mom came upstairs and said,

"Time to get ready for bed."

We brushed our teeth

and put on our pajamas.

Then the doorbell rang.

From downstairs, Mom called out,

"I have to go next door

to help for a minute.

Don't open the door!

Not for anybody!

I'll be back very soon."

"Let's tell some scary stories,"

I said.

"Me first," said Leon.

"What is your story called?"

asked Marcos.

"It's called *Smart Mariette*,"

Leon said. "Listen."

SMART MARIETTE

(Leon's Story)

Mariette's mother and father
were going to a party.

"Come with us," said her father.

"No, Father. I want to stay home."

"Come with us," her mother said.

"There will be songs and dances."

"No, Mother. I will stay at home,"
said Mariette.

So they went to the party alone.

"Don't open the door!

Not for anybody!" they said.

"A goblin could come

and eat you alive.

We will be back by morning."

At midnight, there was a knock

on the door.

Mariette woke up.

Again, there was a knock

on the door.

Mariette got up and looked

out the window.

Standing in the moonlight,

was her best friend, Lisa.

"Are you alone?" Lisa asked.

"Yes, I'm alone," Mariette replied,

opening the door.

"My father and mother went

to a party."

"Good! I'm glad no one else

is home," said Lisa.

"I'll stay the night with you.

Let's take a walk in the jungle.

We could catch some frogs.

I know you like frogs."

The jungle was filled

with noise,

and the croaking of the frogs

was the loudest noise of all.

Lisa caught some frogs

and got very excited.

Crunch! Crunch!

She munched them

as soon as she caught them!

Mariette was scared.

People didn't eat frogs alive –

but goblins did.

Now Mariette knew

that this was not her friend Lisa.

It must be the goblin her parents

had warned her about.

"I have an idea," Mariette said

to the goblin.

"You go one way,

and I'll go another,

so we can catch more frogs.

Let's shout to each other

to say how many we've got."

But when the goblin called,

"How many frogs do you have?"

Mariette replied, "Hush!

You're frightening the frogs,

and I can't catch any."

So the goblin was quiet

and Mariette ran home

as fast as she could.

When she got there,

she climbed to the roof

and hid until morning,

when her parents returned.

Mariette told them everything

that had happened.

"Next time, when we ask you

not to open the door,

you must listen," they said.

Mariette promised she would,

and she did.

"People eating frogs?

"Yuck!" I said.

"They cook them first.

My mom says they taste

like chicken," said Leon.

"Okay, but now I get to

tell a story," I said.

"What is it about?" asked Leon.

"It's about a boy who lived

with a reindeer," I replied.

"The boy had a pet reindeer?"

asked Marcos.

"No. The reindeer took care

of the boy," I said.

"They lived in the woods."

THE WICKED
WOODEN MAIDENS

(My Story)

Once there was a little boy

who lived in a house

with a reindeer.

Every time when the reindeer

went out, he said to the boy,

"Don't open the door!

Not for anybody!

Something terrible

could happen to you."

One day, after the reindeer

had gone to get food,

there was a knock on the door.

"Who's there?" the boy asked.

Outside, sweet voices sang,

"Please, please open the door,

just a wee crack

for one finger. No more."

The boy knew better,

but he was dying to see

who owned those sweet voices.

So he opened the door,

just a teeny, weeny bit.

Instantly, two little white fingers

popped inside.

Then two more, and two more!

Then little white hands

and little white arms.

Before the boy knew

what was happening,

three wicked wooden maidens

had squeezed into the room.

They danced around him,

yelled at him,

and then they dragged him

out of the house

and into the woods.

The boy was frightened

and he screamed,

"Reindeer, Reindeer,

come and help me! Don't delay!

The wicked wooden maidens

are taking me away!"

But the reindeer was too far away

to hear him.

So the little wooden maidens

carried the boy off to their cave.

They teased him

and made strange faces,

but they also gave him lots to eat.

In fact, they stuffed him

with candies and ice cream

all day long.

Every day they pinched him

and said to each other,

"What do you think sisters?

Is he fat enough yet?"

Finally, after many days,

they pricked his finger

to see how fat he was.

"Yum, yum," they said.

Click, clack! They clapped

their wooden hands.

"Let's prepare him for roasting!"

They took off his clothes

and put him in a big buttered pan.

The boy screamed,

"Reindeer, Reindeer come

and help me! Don't delay!

The wicked wooden maidens

are **roasting** *me today!"*

The reindeer was in the woods

searching for the boy

when he heard him calling.

He burst into the cave,

scooped up the boy

with his antlers,

and ran back to their house.

The little boy promised

never, ever to open the door

to strangers again.

And he never did.

"That wasn't very scary,"

Marcos said.

"I know a much scarier story.

Want to hear it?"

"Sure," Leon and I said.

★

EVIL ROCKS

(Marcos' Story)

High in the mountains,

a woman and her daughter

were looking for their lost lamb.

"I'm tired," said the little girl.

"Can we rest?"

38

"You stay here in this little hut

and rest, while I look

a bit further," said her mother.

"Don't open the door!

Not for anybody.

I'll be back soon.

You will be safe here," she said.

But it wasn't safe there.

Nearby, Capusa, the witch,

lived behind two giant rocks.

If you walked between them,

she would close the rocks

and trap you.

These were rocks that

swallowed people.

The little girl was resting

when suddenly, there was

a knock on the door.

"Did you lose your lamb?"

asked a voice outside.

The little girl kept quiet.

"Open the door. I'll show you

where it is," said the voice.

The girl knew she shouldn't

open the door, so she

just peeked through a crack.

She saw an old woman

standing there.

In the distance she could hear

the bleating of her lamb,

so she knew that it was out there.

What she didn't know

was that the old woman

was the witch, Capusa.

The little girl thought,

My mother won't be angry.

She'll be happy I found the lamb!

So the girl opened the door.

"Come with me!"

said the old woman,

and she led the little girl

to that terrible rock place.

"The lamb is there,

just in between those rocks,"

the witch said.

"Go and look!"

The little girl walked

in between the rocks.

And at that very moment . . .

★　★　★

SLEEPOVER

PART 2

"Quiet!" said Leon.

"Do you hear something?"

"What?" Marcos asked.

"Somebody is knocking

on the door.

Listen, do you hear it?"

Knock, knock!

The noise got louder.

Bang! Bang! CRASH! BOOM!

We crawled under the bed.

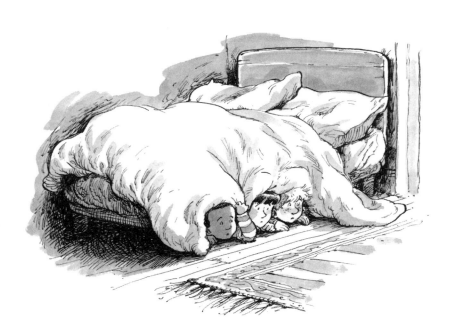

There were footsteps down below!

Then there were footsteps

on the stairs!

And now, there were footsteps

coming along the hallway —

stopping right outside

my room! We crawled

to the farthest corner,

and pretended not to be there.

The door *squ-e-e-e-aked*

as it slowly opened.

Somebody came into the room.

A voice spoke.

"I know you're here!"

Where are you?

WHERE ARE YOU?"

The light came on.

Somebody walked toward my bed

and touched my foot!

"AHH!" I screamed.

"What are you doing there?"

It sounded like my mother.

But I knew better. It was a goblin

disguised as her!

"Couldn't you hear me?"

the voice continued. "I had to

come in through the window.

I forgot the key."

It *was* my mother!

We got out from under the bed.

"You told us not to open the door,"

I said. "Not for anybody."

"That's true," said Mom.

"You did the right thing."

"Now, go to sleep. Goodnight."

"Goodnight," we said,

and climbed under the covers.

Then we went to sleep . . .

but left the lights on.

AFTERWORD

If you're wondering what happened

to the little girl in the Evil Rocks

story, try finishing it yourself.

Think of the best way for the girl

to save herself, and remember,

when the girl escapes the rocks,

all of the other things that were

trapped inside can escape, too.

WHERE THE STORIES COME FROM

Many cultures have stories warning us

not to open the door to strangers.

The Wicked Wooden Maidens

is based on a Bohemian folktale

(sometimes called *Smolicek*).

Smart Mariette is based on

a story from the Guyanas.

The witch in *Evil Rocks*

often appears in Peruvian legends.